one
more
chance

one
more
chance

brian e. miller

One More Chance

ISBN: 978-0-9859131-1-3

Cover and Interior Design by John Takacs. Contact: jjTakacs@gmail.com

Author Website: www.BrianEMillerbooks.com

"Brian has a way of weaving important metaphysical principles into a story that holds your attention…even if you're not quite certain where the story is going. In fact, not knowing where it was going, at first, is one of the reasons 'One More Chance' captured and held my attention. Brian's story-telling skills and eloquence with language are evident in a tale that may remind you a bit of Dickens' 'Christmas Carol', though this tale reveals the struggles taking place globally and individually in the world today."

Beverly Nadler author of *Vibrational Harmony*

"Brian E. Miller is a natural storyteller, he makes it easy to float down the river of the journey he's taking you on. And in 'One More Chance', the water is deceptively deep. Dive in and take a swim, you won't be sorry."

International bestselling author *David Henry Sterry*, author of *Chicken* and *Mort Morte*

"If you like Scrooge and his Ghosts in 'A Christmas Carol'; George Bailey and Clarence the angel in 'It's a Wonderful Life', then you'll enjoy meeting John Meyers and his Old Man in 'One More Chance'.

John Hanc, author of the award-winning memoirs *Not Dead Yet* (with Phil Southerland) and *The Coolest Race on Earth*.

"This is the story of one man's journey of ego transcendence, lessons he learns by being forced to review his history of psychological formation, a journey that brings him freedom."

James Powell author of *Slow Love: A Polynesian Pillow Book*

the
first
chapter

In life, one chance is all we get. Thus the opportunities that arise seem often most important—until a day arrives when all is put in perspective. This is a story of perspective.

John Meyers ends his day as any other, and with the exception of the soft snow falling upon the city street, it is an evening like most. Putting on his long, black wool dress coat covering his tailor-made suit, he smiles to the snow floating past his office window before turning to shut the light. He'll meet his limousine at the curb as always and work on his Blackberry all the way home. An honorable man, a man well respected and a man of great demand in his field, John has always excelled, achieving whatever he put his mind to. He graduated top of his class at Yale and soon after opened his own finance company, which blew to the top of its field in five short years. An avid sailor, he has seen the waters of Asia to the South American Canals and beyond.

John has a beautiful wife, loving children, and five dogs, none of which await him at home, for it's Christmas Eve and all are out shopping and being merry. The dogs are already secured with their upstate caretakers, where they will frolic the snow-covered yard and be cared for over the Christmas break. The entire family leaves for Italy the day after Christmas, a tradition they have maintained for five years now, a different place every year, and often the only time they really get to spend as a family.

"Evening, Mr. Meyers," the driver greets as he opens the limo door.

The contrast of innocent snow-white cotton dots sweeping past the gleaming black of the limo quickly ushers John in.

"Oh, Michael, stop off at Macy's will ya?"

"You got it, Mr. Meyers, a bit of last-minute shopping?"

"That's it."

"You know, Miss Barker could have picked up what you need."

"I don't know what I'm gettin'," John says with a smile.

His assistant, Miss Barker, has taken care of his extensive Christmas list as his pressing engagements of board meetings and the like leave no time for such matters. Yet John resolves every year to buy something with his own hands—a sentimental touch.

They quickly arrive, and as John gets out he hears, "Have Yourself a Merry Little Christmas" grace the loudspeakers outside on the bustling city sidewalk of Macy's, which is decked to the nines with holiday cheer. Reflecting on his childhood, the song brings him back to simpler days. No Blackberry, no Ipad, no seven houses or private jet: just him, his dog Rusty, and mother and sister—a modest life that drove him to reach always for more. John feels content in his success and smiles, as he knows he has come a long way from when he and Rusty would run the yard pretending to be paratroopers in search of Santa's downed sleigh. They rescued him every year. John Meyers, the Savior.

"Sir, a dime, a dollar, anything you can spare on this joyous occasion," a raggedy man with dark, drooping eyes set deep in his dirt-streaked face pleads.

As he holds out a half-crushed cup, his nails blackened with the soot of a rough life reflected in the cracked skin that shakes in his unsteady hands, John drops a twenty-dollar bill in before moving along.

"Thank you!" the man calls out, eyes wide.

After perusing the busy store, John buys some random, quirky, and fun gifts for his son Darryl and daughter Sky. Stopping off at the jewelry section he squeezes past a huddle of tourists toward a necklace that catches his eye behind the glass case.

"Could I see that one?" he asks the woman behind the counter, whose frazzled and curly hair hangs a Santa hat.

"You sure can!" the plump, cheery clerk says, handing him the necklace.

He watches the shimmer of its pearl inlay adorned with iridescent blue streaks that the clerk assures him his wife will love.

"Sold!" John says, handing it back as the woman cracks a crooked, overworked smile.

The ride home is full of answered e-mails and the tickety tock of his Blackberry before finally arriving in the suburbs of his gated home. Michael opens the limo door, and upon standing John hands him an envelope.

"Merry Christmas, Michael, tell the family I said so."

Accepting the envelope Michael knows to be his bonus, he tips his hat with a smile in his heart, "Same to you and yours! Safe travels, Mr. Meyers, see ya in the New Year."

John walks slowly toward the house as a feeling of heaviness overcomes him. *Perhaps that pork chop I had for lunch,* he wonders as he opens the door and enters the barren house. Turning on the stereo, he puts "Have Yourself a Merry Little Christmas" on his Ipod, playing it through the whole house, again bringing him back to his childhood, and before he can take off his coat he grabs his chest with a grimace, falling to the floor. A sharp, stabbing pain pierces his heart as his breathing stops. *A heart attack!* he thinks as he struggles for a last breath, staring at the ceiling.

Flashes of his obituary run through his mind. He will be hailed as a great man, news reports will venerate him, noting his passing and praising his achievements. The eulogy will be eloquent—*but what was it all for—to what end? Have I wasted my life?* The thoughts haunt as darkness overwhelms him.

*the
second
chapter*

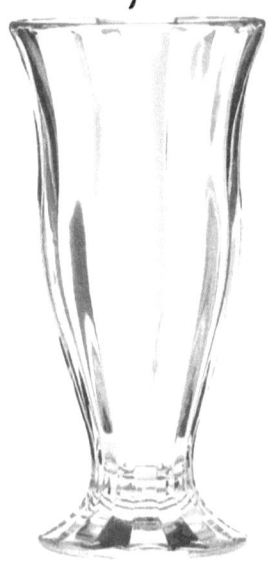

A leaf gently swoops down, softly nestling upon John's face as he opens his eyes in a colorful autumn graveyard. Trees burn bright red as the once lush grass slightly browns and floods the yard, hopping over gravestones and mausoleums covering the hilly land. John squints to see a dog rushing toward him.

"Rusty," he whispers as he makes out his childhood dog.

Looking down at his hands and clothes he notices he is twelve years old again. Rusty pummels him, licking his face as joy gushes from his heart and that old familiar smell of boy's best friend permeates his senses.

"Rusty, oh Rusty, old boy, you're not old at all are you?" he says as Rusty barks back.

His grayish-brown fur hangs like yarn upon a body fit for a mutt. Looking around John laughs in wonder before tackling Rusty, who squirms to break free, and darting off across the yard stops to glance back, waiting for John to give chase. Just before he begins his playful pursuit, he stops. Noticing where he is, a somber mood overwhelms him as he looks down at the gravestone, which reads, "John Meyers 1932-1966."

"Father," he whispers, staring at the large, grey stone now only two years old.

The sun reflects brightly the inlay of carved words, giving John a hypnotic vision that sparks a well of emotions. John remembers how he would visit here often to question and often scold his father for leaving him and his mother and sister.

"You stupid drunk!" he would often cry, cursing the day his father drank so much and after laying ruin to his house and wife's picture-perfect face, got in his car to leave, never returning until he had become a barren man devoid of life, lain out at St. Francis Church that rainy Tuesday of his funeral.

A tear drops down John's cheek as he is distracted by the thought, *If I am twelve, then mom must be home.* Perking up, he yells for Rusty as he begins to bolt for his home, only a few minutes away. Rusty quickly gains speed as they run past the old general store to find Mr. Caruso sweeping up.

"Mr. Caruso?" John yells out, catching his breath, "Ha ha, it's really you!"

"Why yes, who else is gonna sweep this lot?" he answers back.

"It's been so long, you look so, so young."

"You feelin' all right, boy?"

"Ha ha! Oh, Mr. Caruso, you fiery old chap," John says running off as Mr. Caruso stands dumbfounded, broom in hand."

The two-member parade of boy and dog pant back as they burst through the door.

"Mama!?" he yells out.

"Why, John, not so loud, your sister is practicing her notes."

"Oh, Mama!" he yells as he grabs her tight, a tear falling down his cheek.

"John, are you okay? What's the matter, baby?"

Pulling back, he can hear the chop of the old piano being practiced as he looks at his youthful mother. He hasn't seen her since her passing many years ago, a lonely shell of a woman in her final years.

"Mama, I'm sorry."

"For what, John boy?"

As tears stream his face he smiles, "For everything, anything, you're the best Mama a boy could have, you know."

"Oh, John," she says, smiling and pulling away from him as she glances out the window, hoping not to see a police officer nearing the door.

"What happened? You haven't set fire to the woods again have you?"

"No, Mom, just happy to see you."

She gives a laugh of relief as she pats him on the back.

"Well you know, every day I thank God for you and Marissa. Now run along and wash up, dinner's soon, and I need you to set the table."

John runs off into the living room to find Marissa chopping away at the old piano they had bought at the church fair some years back.

"Wow!" He whispers noting the room in amazement before running his fingers on the piano, "What a piece," he says as Marissa stops playing.

"It's a nice piece at that, and I don't care if you don't think so," Marissa says with annoyance.

John remembers teasing her about the old, rickety piano.

"It's a lovely piece," he says staring at her with deep love, "You'll play it well one day," he says noting her persistence that would soon lead her to a career as a music teacher.

Not sure how to react to the endearing comment, she launches into "Twinkle, Twinkle Little Star."

John walks toward the bathroom, in awe of all the wonder of his childhood and begins to wash his dirty hands.

What was I doing today? he thinks, noticing the black nails wrought with dirt. Finishing up, he heads into the kitchen and whistles as he sets the table.

He gives Marissa a darting smile as she comes in to sit.

"Well you're in a good mood," she notes.

"Why wouldn't I be?"

Marissa looks at her mother curiously, who gives her a look back, widening her eyes and tilting her head as to say *let it alone.* You see, at this age John was still a bit bitter about his father's passing: lashing out at school, setting fires, teasing his sister, and often disrespecting his mother. As they sit, he takes a deep breath and suddenly remembers this day. His mother is about to say a prayer and mention his father, when John will promptly lash out and throw a plate, sending the family into hysterics. And what's more, he will scold his mother, blaming her for his father's death.

Oh no, he thinks, *what a foolish boy I was, how fortunate I am to be here to change this.*

Just then he notices an old man in the window outside, looking in as his mother begins.

"Dear Lord..." and to that start the curious man outside waves his finger, lifting John from his childhood body: he can still see the table occupied by him and his family.

No, no, he screams silently, struggling to come back to his body, *I must stop him. He's a foolish, young boy. He doesn't really mean it!* And with that thought he hovers above the table, viewing an angry little boy about to lash out.

No, he doesn't mean it, he yells as he hears *doesn't he?* and all falls black.

*the
third
chapter*

The soft splash of water awakens John's attention to a curious, colored, and wet rock he holds in his young hand. Looking out, he takes in the small expanse of water that makes up the Long Island Sound. Dreamlike, he looks down at his rolled-up jeans as he stands ankle deep in the clear summer water.

"John boy, c'mon, how you gonna learn to fish by lookin' at rocks all day?" he hears the familiar voice behind him as a shiver shoots from his gut to his groin, consuming him before slowly turning.

"Dad?" he whispers as he looks up in trepidation.

"Now pay attention. See, if you loop the line through like so...John? You hearin' me?" his father asks noticing a blank stare on John's face.

"Yes, Pop," he replies, almost completely regressing back to that ten-year-old boy learning to fish on the shore.

"Well then, what did I say?"

"Pop, you loop it like this, and actually it's better if you tie a double stitch. Here, let me see it," young John asks, taking the fishing line, to his father's amazement. "And loop it once more for certitude and wrap the line and there you go," he says, handing it back to his father, who stutters in surprise to the usually submissive John.

"Where'd you learn that?" he asks.

John had become an avid fisher on his sailboat journeys many years later, but it was his father who peaked his interest, in fact, on this very day.

"Oh, you taught me, Pop."

"I never taught you that one," he says, jogging his mind for perhaps a drunken day he doesn't remember.

"Anyhow, let me show you how to cast it."

"I know that."

"Oh you do, do you?"

"I know that you'll show me, I mean," John says, catching himself as he remembers his father's hardheaded temper. He would do anything to avoid his father's scolding.

"Here, like this," he places the rod in young John's hands.

He looks out onto the sound, it seems smaller than he had remembered. Feeling the strong, rough hands of his father, the smell of cigarettes and booze bring a comfort to John, and for the first time he feels the great love and admiration he'd had for his father as a boy. His father was a god to him, seemingly knowing everything. A tear falls down John's cheek as they rhythmically sway the rod back and forth.

"Back like a tree in the breeze and a gust to the thrust and release."

The zing of the reel casts the line far as John looks up to his father with a smile. He misses his father deeply—a strange missing that seems to be suppressed in years of anger.

"Don't look at me, boy, reel!"

John reels and reels, and as the line tightens he realizes he is stuck. His father lights a cigarette, dragging the smoke into his tanned face adorned with black, curly hair. His father was a good looking man, although at this point the booze had begun to take its toll, tightening his face and often dragging red lines around his light-brown eyes.

"Reel, John Boy, reel!" he yells.

John feels the anxiety of seeking his father's approval and notices the line is indeed stuck.

"Give me that," he says grabbing the line from John and as he jerks the rod, trying to set the line free, he squints out the smoke from the cigarette that dangles from his mouth.

John looks up as that familiar feel of terror overcomes him.

"Ahhh!" his father scolds, pulling a knife from his side holster to cut the line.

"Sorry, Pop, I..."

"No, no, sorry doesn't fix things, John," he says as he rethreads the rod in silence.

John remembers that cold shoulder his father would give. Usually an ambiguous line like *Sorry doesn't fix things*, followed by silent incertitude. *Is he angry at me or what?* This was commonplace.

"Can I try again?" he asks, knowing he can cast twice as far and in fact is a much more skillful fisher than his father.

If he didn't get caught in the moment, the line wouldn't have stuck, but he remembers this is exactly what happened that day.

"No, not today. Watch how a man does it, John Boy."

And to that end, John spends the rest of the day watching his father cast line after line, cigarette upon cigarette, beer after beer, before finally a snag.

"Oh boy!" he says, resting his cigarette in his mouth as he reels rigorously, finally pulling in a large bass which flops and struggles on the sand.

John remembers feeling both excited and sorry for the fish as his father removes the hook.

"Now that's how a man does it, boy," his father says, eyes glazed from the empty cans that pollute the cooler.

"Dinner!" John exclaims as his father laughs.

As he puts the fish in the bucket, the sun dances it's final steps, pouring a pinkish hue across the skyline, highlighting long clouds like thick fingers about to close down upon the world. As John carries the cooler and rod and begins to follow his father toward the wood stairs that lead up the dune, he watches as water splashes from the bucket that holds the fish, it's tail hangs out too large for even the largest bucket they own. A strange feeling of love and admiration for his father overcomes him as he looks over to a man casting out to sea in his waders and tan fishing cap. John watches him for a moment, and suddenly he turns and smiles as if he felt John watching him.

The old man from the window at mother's, he thinks.

The man's smile stretches wrinkles across his face as a profound stare with his deep, light-blue eyes again pulls John from his childhood body. He observes his father and young John as they top the stairs, catching their breath. Young John runs his hand along the scales of the fish in the bucket.

"One day you'll catch one like this," his father says.

Young John smiles. "I love you, Dad," he says.

"Alright, let's get home so your mother can cook this baby up."

John's observance pulls further away.

      He never told me he loved me, never once, he thinks as he pulls so far above them that young John and his father look like ants.

The now tangerine sky consumes his consciousness and is all he can see. In a blink, all falls silent and blissful.

the
fourth
chapter

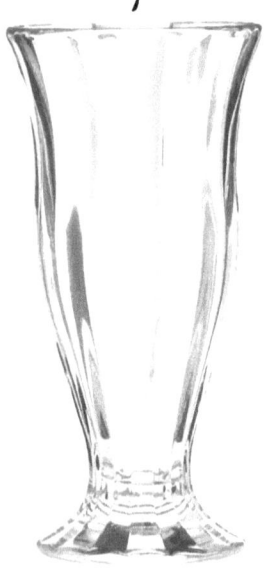

Opening his eyes, John sits at his desk in New York. Feeling faint for a moment as he comes to, he thinks, *Was this a dream? Did I fall asleep?* These thoughts are quickly dispelled as he looks at the calendar: February 12, 2006.

"Mr. Meyers, your son is in on the phone," the intercom on his desk alerts.

"Thank you, Rita," he says into the phone's intercom before picking up.

"Darry! How'd it go?" he asks.

"Oh, Dad, it's a nightmare, she said if I don't ace the test I'll get a D, that'll kill my chances at Yale."

"Well should have thought of that before spending all your time at those parties," John fires back.

"Dad, I'm in college. There are parties, and I don't spend all my time partying like you and Mom assume. She's a tough teacher. It's just my schedule and..."

"Darry, just ace the test—right?"

"Right," Darry says uncertainly.

"Darry you're gonna face tough teachers at Yale. Life is full of walls to hurdle, obstacles to complete. You think my business flourished by me hanging on the beach? It took determination, persistence, and when a wall presented itself I climbed it and never gave up until all those walls were behind me. And soon I became an expert wall climber," he laughs.

"Yeah, thanks, Dad," Darryl says uncertainly.

"Son, never give up. You'll never fail if you never give up," John says, noting a reminder of a meeting, which pops up on his computer screen.

"Dad, you're right, I'm gonna ace that test! I love you Dad, thanks!"

"All right, now get cracking on those books, I gotta run, got another wall to climb," he says noting the importance of the meeting.

"Bye, Dad."

"Talk to you soon, Darry."

Hanging up the phone, he realizes the 2006 John is on autopilot. Even though he occupies his body, he is sort of just in observance. Standing by his window, he packs his briefcase. He looks out the window across to the building on the other side of the street and squints to make out a man seemingly staring at him.

I never told him I loved him, he thinks as he frantically stares at the man, whom he now realizes is the same man on the beach and in his mother's window.

"Who are you?" he says out loud before turning to call Darryl to tell him he loves him. *Why did I never tell him this?* he thinks as he lifts from his body.

"No, no, not yet, I must call him!"

He looks back at the man in the window, who curiously seems much closer.

"Who are you?" he asks to a smiling old man standing static in a double-breasted suit.

His awareness grows hazy as he watches his younger self head out of the office for a meeting as the world fades away.

the
fifth
chapter

A faint sound of a train whistle brings his attention to the rug on which he sits with a toy fire truck on the floor of this vastly unfamiliar home.

"Come on, John," a woman's voice calls.

Looking up, he recognizes his grandmother, younger than he has ever seen her.

"Grandma?" he asks in amazement.

"Watch it, John, you're father just pulled up, get over to the table."

Looking out the window, he notices his grandfather and quickly realizes he is in his father's body, as a boy. Sitting in amazement at the table, set for three, he watches as his grandmother mixes up a gin and tonic.

The door squeaks open and then closes. He can hear his grandfather take off his coat and walk toward the dining room. As he enters the room he smacks his foot on the fire truck.

"God damn it! John, are you still playing with toys? Clean this mess up!" he yells as fear wells up in John's body and an uncontrolled tremble overwhelms him.

"I told him that," his mother says with drink in hand, seemingly more fearful than John as his father grabs the drink in discontent.

"There's a war going on, and you two spend all

day playing and what?"

"No, dear, I made dinner, John was at school."

"Yeah, Dad, I made a bridge out of sticks today," John says as the words oddly just come out of him. He observes his father's young body.

"Well that's just grand," his father says condescendingly. It's obvious he is in a bad mood.

"Where's my dinner?" he demands.

"About five minutes, dear," she says, cracking the stove to check where the wonderful smell of chicken and potatoes is streaming from. A sigh of discontent overcomes him.

"Dad, wanna see my bridge?" John says, rising up and running for his room as his father rolls his eyes at his mother.

"Jack, he is just a boy, and you're his father. Show some semblance of concern," his mother beckons as John leaves the room to get his school project.

"A boy, he's damn near thirteen years old, still playing with toys. When I was thirteen I was providing for my family."

"Times were different," she says.

"Damn right they were, and my father had me out cutting wood for sale. Had he not, we would have starved."

John enters back into the room with the rickety model bridge made from sticks he had gathered from their yard.

"John may grow up to be a bridge builder."

"A bridge designer, Mom, maybe an engineer," John says proudly wearing a leather aviator hat.

"Boy, what is that on your head?" his father asks.

"Oh this? It's an official bomber hat, Dad. You like it?" he asks placing the bridge on the table.

"And where did you get the money to buy that?" he asks, looking at his wife, who shakes her head no.

"Mr. Coen gave it to me. He said it makes me official, and that one day I can fly for our country."

"Mr. Coen! What did I tell you 'bout hanging around that Jew's shop?"

"Well, I, I—"

"Now, you give it back to him. We don't need any handouts from the Coens."

"Now, Jack, he's only being nice on the count that John listens to his stories," his mother defends.

"Stories? Now you listen and listen good. I don't want you filling your head with that Kike's nonsense. You hear?"

"Pa, he only means well."

Just then Jack stands up, grabbing the hat from his head.

"You gonna be an aviator, a bridge builder, a fireman. Boy, wake up! Pull your head from the clouds."

John begins to cry as he stands behind his mother.

"Jack, please," his mother pleads as Jack stuffs the hat in the garbage.

"And what's more, if you have so much time to be hanging out at the Coen's shop, maybe it's time you work, pull some damn weight around here instead of playing with toys and constructing silly bridges."

"It was for school, Dad," John cries.

"You can't hide behind your mother your whole life!" he yells out as he smashes the bridge to pieces.

The air of anger grows thick.

"Get in your room, John!" he demands.

"But, Pa?"

"Get in your room!" he demands again as a knock on the door diverts his attention.

John stands, and as his mother hugs him, Jack answers the door. The mutter of conversation can be heard between Jack and the visiting salesman.

"Go on, John, I'll save you some dinner. Let me

calm your father down."

John goes off to his room upstairs, and as his father
sends the salesman away, John looks out the window
to see the old salesman look up. It's the blue-eyed man
again. He smiles and waves as John presses his face
against the window, swollen with tears in the stillness of
his room. He begins to pull from his father's body.

*Love was not a word in the father–son vocabulary
for my father,* he thinks as the evening sky darkens and
all falls black.

the
sixth
chapter

"Brentwood. Next stop, Central Islip. This is the train to Ronkonkoma. Ronkonkoma will be the last and final stop on this train."

John hears the conductor over the loudspeaker as he opens his tired eyes and looks at his watch. It reads almost half past eleven. Another late night ride home from New York.

Must be early in my career, he thinks as later he would be riding in a limo or staying in his apartment on the upper-east side on his many nights working late. *Here I am again,* he thinks noting the near barren midweek train.

This journey of bountiful emotions is growing stranger as John swaps from body to body.

"Central Islip, this is Central Islip, next and last stop is Ronkonkoma, all passengers must exit the train at Ronkonkoma, train goes to the yard from there," the conductor blurts out as John tries to remember the last time he has ridden the train.

Watching the dark, sleepy town cruise past the window, he wonders what this is all for.

Am I dead? Dreaming? Perhaps a case of delusional hallucinations due to food poisoning? he wonders.

"Ronkonkoma, this is the last stop on the train. Please gather all your belongings, train goes to the yard from here."

As the train pulls into the station it hisses, ending with a ding to open the doors. John feels a heavy burden of mental exertion as he drags on to his car.

"There she is," he says, standing in front of his 1976 banana-yellow Chevy Chevette.

He takes a deep breath of wonder as he opens the door and sitting on the plaid seat that covers the tan leather outskirts, turns the key. She starts right up.

"Old faithful," he says with a laugh.

Looking down at the newspaper he must have left on the seat in the morning rush not to miss the train, it reads: President Halts Grain to Russia Following Afghanistan Invasion.

Looking at the date on the paper, he sees it was printed in 1980. He smiles, realizing he and his wife live in a small, one-bedroom apartment not far from there. Putting on the radio, the song "Happy Christmas War is Over" comes in midsong. He realizes that John Lennon will be slain in a couple of months as he turns up the volume and pulls off in the cold of night. As he drives down the street, he grows giddy at his time travels and begins to wonder what he is doing here, or anywhere he's been going. He feels there are lessons to be learned, perhaps things to be changed. Feeling he is not in control of this journey he pushes down on the gas pedal, hurrying home to see his old apartment. Finally pulling up in the silence of night, he turns off the engine, deepening a stillness pervaded only by the gentle whisper of wind in the trees telling him to be quiet as he nears the door.

"Shhhhh," the trees warn as he enters the dark house.

It is a common night coming home to his wife asleep, and as he wonders at the old apartment, he remembers waking before sunrise and arriving home late at night, often not seeing Mallory. But it's what he had to do so that he could spend more time with her and future children. Of course now he was aware of an ironic twist: that "future" family time had never seemed to be available, with the exception of the occasional Sunday or vacation after Christmas.

But I would have retired, sold most of the business soon, and been able to live out my days spending copious amounts of time with my wife and children—but the heart attack, he thinks standing in the threshold watching his sweet Mallory sleeping soundly.

A vague glow of moonlight illuminates the otherwise dark room.

Oh, Mallory, he thinks, *you were never second best. Everything I did was for you.*

He thinks of how his death would leave her devastated and alone. Taking off his clothes, he climbs into bed with underwear and t-shirt and holds Mallory's young body close.

"Hi, honey," she whispers with a groggy voice.

"I love you so much, baby," he whispers in her ear.

"I love you too, honey," she whispers back, half dreaming.

Turning to the clock, he turns off the alarm, then holds Mallory tight and drifts off to sleep as they lie in union.

the
seventh
chapter

"John, John! wake up!" Mallory says frantically.

John springs awake, "What is it?" he asks, rubbing his eyes, realizing it is still 1980, the very next morning.

"John, your alarm never went off, you're gonna be late!"

John smiles, knowing he shut off the alarm so he could see her in the morning, whether he would have been conscious of it or not, in the hopes he may be able to set some sort of trend for the future.

"Baby, you are so beautiful," he says as he looks over at the bureau mirror, rubbing his young face and laughing.

"What is so funny, you are late, you know."

"No no, I'm gonna spend the day with you. Thought we could go to that place we used to, that diner on 111," he says.

"You sure, John?" she asks, curious about his laxity.

"Never been more sure of anything in my life, Mallory. I love you very much. You're number one to me," he says.

"Oh, John, I know," she replies as she hugs him.

"I'll make some coffee," she says.

As she leaves the room he gets up, wandering around the small apartment with a permanent grin.

I want to stay right here, he thinks. "Whoever is in control, please can I stay here and start over?" he pleads.

"What's that, honey?" Mallory asks from the small kitchenette.

"Oh nothing," he replies as he looks out into the late morning sun at all the old cars meandering down the block.

Noticing the mailman as he nears the house, he recognizes him to be the old, blue-eyed man and knows he will soon leave.

No! he thinks as he runs out the door in his boxers and t-shirt toward the man who stands putting mail in a box starring at John as he nears him.

"Who are you?" he yells. "Please, I must stay here."

The old man smiles with compassion as John begins to lift from his body once again.

"No, please," he pleads, now observing himself walking back to the apartment with mail in hand.

As he enters the door, Mallory stands holding out the phone, "John, it's Michael," Mallory says with concern as John grabs the phone.

"Hello," he says confused.

"John, what gives, we need you here, the Hillman account, did you forget?" Michael stresses on the other end of the phone.

"Michael, stall the meeting, I must have over-slept, I'm leaving now, tell 'em I had a family emergency. No, tell 'em someone died, I don't know."

As John observes his neurotic old self, he pulls further away, trying to grab at Mallory, who looks at his frantic younger self with confusion.

"Someone did die," he hears, "it was you," he hears as all falls black.

the
eighth
chapter

Hovering above a blur of what looks like a pond glinting in the sun reflecting vibrant reds and oranges, John descends and slips into a much younger body as he sits fishing with his old college buddy Bill. Coming into his body, he realizes the beauty of a fall day as yellow leaves float atop this small fishing pond of Baldwin Park. Still upset from the last experience he sits in ill content.

"John, you alright man?" Bill asks with concern.

"Uh, what? Uhm, yeah," John replies in a stupor.

"I lost you there for a second," Bill says with a smile.

"What?" John asks.

"You were explaining about the company, then nothing, blank stare buddy. You and Liz take that acid again last night?"

"Uh, no, no, not at all," John says, laughing at the crazy experience he once had with his friend Liz on an experimental acid trip. "Bill!" he says, laughing.

"Anyway, John, something I need to tell you."

"What's that, Bill?" John says, noting the old peace he would feel when he and Bill would come to fish Baldwin pond nearly every week this fall.

"I'm leaving school, John," Bill says seriously.

John remembers this day. Bill and he had been in talks

of opening a financial company all through college. John again comes out of his body in observance of the scene.

"What? Very funny, Bill."

"No, I am dead serious, John."

"You have a year left, why would you go and do a stupid thing like that? I'm not partnering with someone who has no college degree, Bill," he says jokingly.

"That's the thing, John, I don't wanna partner. No offense. I don't want to do the corporate thing. I'm only here because my father endowed the university. I'm following his dreams, not mine," Bill says.

John remembers the anger and betrayal he felt that day.

"Bill, what about us, our dreams?" he pleads.

"That's your dream, John, and you chose it, but I can't. I don't know," Bill casts out to the pond as silence falls over them both.

"Bill, don't be ridiculous. You're finishing school. What you need to do is stop hanging around that hippie Mark," John laughs.

"Jesus, you sound like my father."

"Well he's a wise man," John touts.

"He's a miserable old fool is what he is, and if he has his way I'll be just like him."

"Bill, how am I going to start the company without you?" John asks.

"You mean, without my father's money?" Bill says directly.

"No, Bill, you're my partner," John says covering his obvious lie.

"John, you're smart, you'll do it with or without me."

"What the hell are you gonna do?" John asks sternly.

"I don't know, I'm thinking of going to Tibet."

"Tibet!" John laughs. "For what?"

"I've been studying a lot of Eastern philosophy. It makes so much sense to me. You ever heard of Alan Watts?"

"No," John says, uninterested.

"I wanna go to Japan, Tibet, India. I want to find my true purpose, John, I feel a deeper calling for me than just a shallow financial company."

"Shallow?" John says, looking at Bill now with disgust.

"No, not shallow, that came out wrong," Bill retracts.

"Yeah," John says unamused.

"John, that is your bliss. Follow it, but it's not mine. I saw a lecture by Joseph Campbell on campus, and he said, 'When you follow your bliss doors will open where you would not have thought there were doors. And where there would not be a door for anyone else.' This is my bliss, John," Bill says passionately.

"Bill, look, I understand, but this is the real world, not some fantasy novel. You don't wanna end up regretting your life, haphazardly floating around like a hippie."

"John, I feel a deeper cause in me to do what I must. I am not debating with you. I am telling you. I leave next week for India."

"What? Are you serious?" John stands up from the rock where he has been sitting pond side. "Well, that's just perfect! Look, Bill, if you leave, our partnership is through. No coming back and pleading your way back in. I don't need some whiney little rich boy who can't make up his mind as a partner."

As John says that, he enters back into his body, as he has just witnessed what a fool his anger has made him.

"Whiney little rich boy, huh?" Bill says, shaking his head.

"No, Bill, please, I didn't," John tries to apologize for a younger, more vigilant, and angry John he just observed.

"You said your piece, and I mine. You gave your ultimatum, and now that we're on the honesty track, I have something to say to you, John. Beware of your ego.

Do you want to own this company for power and money or to bring joy to the world, to make a positive difference? Having wealth and riches is fine. It's the intention behind it that will often make it stink, and yours smells like the depths of the sewer."

Bill turns and walks away.

"Bill, come back." John says, grabbing his tackle box and following his perturbed friend.

Once again he sees the old man sitting patiently on a bench that Bill walks toward, leaving the park. John pretends not to notice him, but it's no use. He draws once again from his body, observing himself in hot pursuit toward Bill, and as he puts a hand on Bill's shoulder Bill turns to look at John.

"What is it, John?" Bill asks impatiently.

"The sewer, ay? Well I'll have you know that Miguel and I have been talking, and we think you're not man enough for our firm anyhow," John says out of anger.

"John, this is silly. You're a silly child of a man right now still trying to prove something to your father."

To that end John punches Bill in the mouth. Bill's head lashes back and as he stands with a bloody lip, he says, "I'm sorry it had to come to this," and walks away, leaving an insecure and confused John on the field.

He would never see Bill again after that day, and as the

old man walks along the field looking at Bill, John ascends high above the park and again bears witness to the darkness all around him.

"Why am I seeing this?" he asks. "Please, I can't anymore," he pleads. "Please show me happy times," he begs.

the
ninth
chapter

Cars blow horns as John whips down the expressway in the rain, cutting people off to get to the exit and finally to the hospital. He slowly enters his body again as he hurdles through the main units of a brightly lit hospital.

"Mallory Meyers, I'm here to see Mallory Meyers" he pants to the receptionist as she fingers through a stack of papers on a clipboard, searching for the patient.

"She's in childbirth," she says with a smile.

"I know, I'm the father," he yells as she directs him where to go.

He remembers this nervous excitement as he sprints the bright, cold hallway, arriving at the room devoid of his wife and newborn child.

"Can I help you, sir?" a nurse asks.

"I'm looking for my wife, Mallory Meyers."

"Oh yes, we just brought her up to her room in maternity, third floor. Congratulations, Mr. Meyers."

"Thank you," he says as he makes his way to the elevator.

Coming to the quiet maternity ward he enters her room to find her beaming with joy holding their newborn son.

"Baby, I am so sorry. I came as fast as I could."

"Shhh, John, look," she says, smiling to the newborn with eyes closed, fast asleep.

John sits on the bedside and kisses Mallory on the forehead as a tear trickles down his cheek.

"Here, hold him," she says, handing the soft, bundled, baby boy over. His smell is new, soft, and delicate.

"Daryl," he whispers. "I promise to love you. I love you so much, and even if I hadn't told you, I meant it everyday," John says.

"John, he's only been in this world a few hours," Mallory laughs. "I wish your mother were here to see him," Mallory says as John thinks about his mother, who at this point had recently passed, and he begins to sob. Mallory softly takes Daryl back.

"John, I love you."

"I love you too, my princess."

"John."

"Yes, dear?"

"I am starving," Mallory says as they both have a laugh.

"I am sure you are, I'll go get you something."

"I've been craving cheeseburgers for two days," Mallory says with a chuckle.

"Cheeseburger it is, with all the fixings. I'll be

back in a bit." he says as he heads out the door into the hallway, bumping into a doctor in a white coat.

"Excuse me, sir," he says before noticing it's the old man.

"Say, what gives? Who are you?" he asks while grabbing the man's coat.

Pulling back, the silent old man waves him on and again he ascends from his body, leaving the hospital window, floating high up in the sky. Quickly his awareness skyrockets down through a wooded path. Streaking trees mesh past before arriving at a modest community where he enters a window. A bright pulse of light blinds him for a moment before his focus comes into view and he finds himself in a small living room where he watches himself stand rubbing his stubbled face.

"I'm not thrilled, I'll say that," he hears his mother say as he quickly turns to find his mother standing with a saddened face.

"Mom," he says, noticing where he is.

"John, not like this, I can't," his mother says, referring to the community home they are checking out, where he would eventually put her to live out her last two years.

"Hello?" he hears a voice from the front call out.

"Marissa, dear, we are back here," her mother answers as Marissa enters the living room.

"Hey, guys, sorry. I hit some traffic," she says, coming to hug her mother.

"So, John and I were just discussing how we don't like it here. Why don't I stay with you and Fred, Marissa?" her mother says insecurely.

"Mom, we talked about this," Marissa says with compassion.

"This place has it all. Look! Bingo, movie night, gentle yoga," John says holding a pamphlet as his mother rolls her eyes, unamused.

"Mom, you'll be fine. We'll be here all the time. You can come see us, too. We're not far; this place is cute, too," Marissa says, perusing the hallway into the small kitchen.

"I don't know why I can't stay at my house. I mean, it ought to be my decision. You know I am your mother."

"It was your decision, Mom. You are so far away. We want you to be closer, and with all the fainting episodes, Mom, it's not safe," John says now just in observance of his body.

"Well, maybe if you visited more than once a year, I mean I'm just saying."

"Ma, you're gonna love it here, once you settle in. I promise," Marissa says with her hands gently on her mother's shoulders.

"I suppose," she says, feeling defeated.

"Come on, let's go to lunch," John calls out from the kitchen.

"Let me use the bathroom," their mother says, slowly making her pale, fragile body move toward the bathroom.

"She won't be happy here, I know it." Marissa says as John's awareness observes the situation without control.

"She'll be fine," John contends nonchalantly.

"Yeah, that sounded heartfelt," Marissa dismisses.

"Well, what's our alternative? You want her to live with you?" John retorts.

"I want her to be happy, John, it's all I want. You want her to be safely stowed away, like always."

"Why would you say a stupid think like that? She's my mother too. I love her," he says, softening his voice.

"You don't always act like it. I mean you can pick up the phone."

"I call her. How would you know?"

"She tells me, John. She misses you and the kids. She loves you, and she wants a son, not a bank account."

"Yea, well lucky for us all, I have the money to

pay for this place, because it is not cheap."

"Yea, so that's it? Is she a mother or a dollar sign? Let me ask you something, John. When did you start seeing Mom as a liability? I mean she can't make you money, so might as well put her aside," Marissa says in an obvious venting of much unresolved past issues.

"You're being a fool. Lower your voice," John says sternly.

"Or what? Or Mom may find out how you feel?"

"You have no idea how I feel."

"You're right, John. No one does, but actions give a good description. It's no wonder Mallory says you're like the invisible man half the year."

"Leave her out of this. Look—"

"What are you two arguing about?" their mother says, coming out of the bathroom. "Look, I know I'm old and difficult and stubborn and Lord knows what else, but above all, one thing will never change, I love you two and there is never a reason for you to bicker. Life's too short. I'll get by fine here I'm sure. Now you two make up. I don't need you to argue on account of me."

"Oh, Mom, it wasn't about you," Marissa says.

"My eyes may have gone to pieces, but my ears are as sharp as the day you were born, lil' missy."

John swallows a lump in his throat composed of

guilt and anger.

"So that settles it. We'll sign the papers then." John says.

Looking at John through her thick glasses, she smiles a smile that can only mask a frown.

"John, you do what you feel is right. I always told you to follow your heart, and a mother can show the way, but it's up to you to walk that way. So you do what's right. Feel it baby. I trust you," she says.

"Okay then, the choice is made, let's go to lunch," John comments as his mother's eyes look down to the floor in suppressed sadness.

John's awareness begins to pull away once again as they leave the small condo, and a thump drops his heart.

I didn't listen to my heart, he thinks as all goes black and silent. "What is this all for?" he asks in the silence as once again his eyes open and he is seated at a diner booth.

Looking around, he notices it is the 1950's. He looks over at the mirrored wall to his left, and oddly he is the full-grown John in a suit and tie. Snow falls gracefully outside, and he realizes where he is. It's his favorite childhood diner. Fond memories are all he has of this place.

"What can I get ya, good lookin'?" the waitress asks.

"Oh, like a, you still have those strawberry

shakes?" he asks, feeling giddy.

"Still have 'em darlin'. Unless they melted in this heat wave," she says looking out at the snow that seems to be falling harder by the moment.

"I'll take one," John resolves.

Just then the chains of the doorbells ring out and a man enters wearing a long wool coat covered with snow. The diner is empty with the exception of a couple far off at the other end. As the newcomer hangs up his hat and coat John notices it's the old man, and butterflies well up in his stomach. Walking toward him, John is speechless and still. The old man comes to sit directly across from John in the booth, and they stare eye to eye.

"What? Who? What is all this?" John asks.

The old man smiles as the waitress brings the strawberry shake in a tall glass that flares out at the top, just as he remembered it.

"What can I get for you, handsome? You need a menu?" she asks the old man, who shakes his head no.

"One of those would be perfect," he says.

"You got it. Strawberry shake," she confirms.

"What gives, old man?" John asks.

"Easy there, you're no spring chicken yourself. In fact you just had a heart attack."

"Is that what this is? Am I dead?" John asks, concerned.

"Not exactly, John. Not exactly," the old man says softly.

"Who are you? I mean, what are you?" John asks.

"All in good time, but just tell me how have you enjoyed your journey so far?" the old man asks.

"I'm not going to lie, it's very fantastic but very difficult to swallow. Why have you shown me these difficulties? There has been much joy in my life, no?"

The old man just smiles.

"Are you God?" John asks in a whisper.

"Not exactly," the old man says as the waitress brings the shake.

"Here you go, handsome. Enjoy."

"Thank you," the old man replies.

"Go on, John, before it melts," the old man directs.

John gulps a few sips of his shake. "Wow, amazing! Just like I remembered. How did you do this?" he asks, amazed.

"Do what?"

"This. Recreate this place. It's exact to the t, and all the other things. I mean fishing with my father."

"I didn't do any of this. It all happened. Time, John. It's a structure of odd proportions on this Earth. It's all happening now, and you bring it up.

You can recreate your version of it. This diner is your version, and a grand version at that."

"You look familiar," John says. "Do I know you? Did I work with you?" John asks, examining the old man.

"Not exactly," he replies.

"Not exactly," John mimics. "So what are you, like, my angel who is going to help me see the errors of my ways, like in *It's A Wonderful Life?*"

"Well, John—"

"Let me guess, not exactly?" John interrupts.

"Exactly," the old man smiles before drinking his shake.

"John, do you remember this day?"

John looks around.

"Not exactly," he says with a smirk. He then sees his younger self sitting alone at a booth, about thirteen years old, drinking a strawberry shake.

"Yes, yes I do. I'd come here after school."

"Yes, John, it's a happy place for you. Today you were bullied in the park as you were building an igloo."

"Yes, I remember," John laughs.

"Yes, well you remember where you got the money for that shake?"

John jogs his memory. "Of course, I struggled free and punched that big brute Maxwell in the gut and took his money," John laughs. "Oh and he is waiting for me in that parking lot with his friends," he says as he looks out the window.

"Yes, he is, isn't he? Lucky shot I guess on old Maxwell, and now you'll pay the price," the old man says.

"Yeah, but I remember enjoying the hell out of that milkshake."

"But when the diner closed and you walked home, you would get a beating like none other you had ever received."

"Oh yes, oh, so what? Can I go out there and toss old Maxwell one for lil' old Johnny Boy?"

"Not exactly, John. John, things have causes and effects in our lives, and things happen where we often think they are bad, but perhaps it's exactly what we needed to learn or forgive, to grow."

John is fixated on his youthful self, in awe as he watches young John confidently down the shake.

"And so am I to learn that all this pain I've seen has a reason," John asks.

"You're to learn that you create your reality, John. Nothing is inherently right or wrong with our struggles or actions. Right might be defined as an action that brings joy and happiness to you and others. Then wrong would be something that creates suffering in you or others, all just labels, John. All along, the reality is that, it's all perfect outside of our delusions of right and wrong. I am trying to tell you that much of the suffering you created for yourself and others was not what you truly wanted in your heart, yet you created it anyway."

"I was just a boy," John defends.

"Yes, and you seemed never to grow out of that, because it only got worse as you aged."

"So what's the point? What's done is done, right? Now I feel bad. I never meant to hurt anyone."

"No, you did not. You were blindly led by your delusions of greed, jealousy, anger, and so forth, and so you never honored your mother's wish to follow your heart."

"No one every taught me how," John says.

"And what if you could go back and allow your heart, your truths to decide as opposed to your fear-driven, ego-mad mind? Would you take the challenge?"

"Of course I would! Please let me do this."

Sitting among two empty shake glasses clouded with a pink strawberry hue, the waitress clears them away. "Get you anything else?"

"No thank you," the old man says as she drops the check facedown.

"Have a warm one, boys," she winks and walks off, as John searches for cash.

"You don't have any money, John. In fact, you are not really here. We are sort of just in your mind. It's a bit complicated. You need not worry about the details. Come," the old man says, getting up and walking toward his coat and hat.

He hands John his coat and hat, and as he begins to put them on, he observes young John anxiously looking out the window and walks over to him. "Hey kid," he says.

"Yes?" young John replies, turning, strawberry shake dried to the edges of his mouth, his warm and glowing cheeks contrasting the cold outside.

"Kick the big one in the nuts, then run fast. Rex is the only one who can catch ya."

"Thanks sir, but how'd you know they were waitin' for me?" young John asks.

John smiles at the old man with a quick glance as the old man continues to put on his coat.

"Say, maybe you can help me out?" young John asks.

"No, boy, we must be moving along," the old man says.

"Come on, I mean maybe just this once," John pleads.

The old man gives a look of disapproval as he nods him near the door.

Before John walks out of the door he turns back, "Oh, and kid, Yahoo stock, listen to Mike on that one. You'll know what I mean when it comes up."

"Yahoo stock?" young John says, confused as John nods, eyes wide with a smile, pulling out of the door into the heavy snowfall of the early, dark evening.

"John, there is a catch. As you go into this, you can never let anyone know you are aware of what you are aware of now, or else it will all reset back to how it is. This means no stock tips."

The old man stops for a moment to a smiling shrugging John before he goes on.

"And also, you must do only what your heart wants to say and do, no matter how hard, or else it will default back. Can you do this?"

"I can, old man. What's your name anyway?" John asks.

"Old Man will do for now," he says with a smile as they walk off.

John is amazed and wonders at the old cars and trucks exactly as he remembered.

Looking over at the rough kids awaiting his younger self, he asks, "Have we started yet?"

"Not yet."

"Oh, okay, one second," John says, going over to the three kids who stand impatiently rubbing there boots in the snow as if looking cool is their full-time business.

Walking past the three boys smoking cigarettes awaiting a young him, he hears, "He gotta come out sometime," as the boy spits, "and when he does..."

To that end John looks over at them.

"Excuse me, Maxwell?" he asks.

"Yeah, who wants to know?" Maxwell asks puffing up his chest.

"Your mother doesn't love you," he says.

"What? Fuck your mother, old man."

"Yeah," the ruckus of boys stirs.

"John, rule number two," the old man scolds.

"You said we hadn't started yet."

"Well, we start now, let's go."

"Yeah, you better before we show you how much our fists love you," one boy yells out, flicking his cigarette at John.

John laughs and smiles. "Poor Maxwell," he says as the snow seems to come down now in sheets, and all falls completely white.

*the
tenth
chapter*

John comes to and his focus sharpens as he holds a wrench in a dark basement.

"John, I got it. Ready?" his pudgy friend beckons, spinning a wheel on his inverted bicycle.

I am twelve again, he thinks as he looks around the basement where he and his friend Jim would play for countless hours in imagination, a thousand memories flood in as he stares in wonder.

Jim flips the bike over, where he had just put a new tube in and opens the wooden door of the basement before carrying his bike up the stairs. John gives a quick glance into the basement before closing the door behind him. The boys get on their bikes as the crisp autumn air swoops leaves from the trees. He remembers how they'd ride for miles on journeys to nowhere. He remembers wonderful memories of how wild their imaginations would be, and John also remembers how Jim would be teased and how he would do nothing about it in fear of the same. He always made an insecure effort to be accepted by the other boys he would often play with outside of his time with Jim. He would even secretly make fun of Jim and divulge information Jim had secreted to him for cheap laughs and minor acceptance.

"Where we going, John?"

"The trails, we'll ride to the other end," John says as the words roll out unconsciously.

And as they ride off, John remembers exactly this day.

He is going to lead Jimmy into the woods, where three boys await him to beat him up for no particular reason at all except that he is heavy and insecure. This premeditated plan had taken place on the street before John had gone over to Jim's. He ran into Tommy McSimpon and Jared Bower, and in an attempt to cover up where he was going he agreed to the devious plan of ambush. The fact was that John loved to hang out with Jim. They had great fun. They'd call themselves the double J's, and even made paper badges and membership cards. Their closeted best friendship would prove a fraud today as John led him to those woods. Although Jim would never know the plot and John's involvement, because John would pretend to flee as well, John felt that deep down Jim knew and their friendship grew apart after that day.

John digs his foot into his peddle, activating the brake and dragging the tire to swoop out to a stop, barricading Jim, "On second thought, let's ride up to Mr. Thompson's shop and get some candy."

"Oh yea," Jim says as his eyes light up, and to that end they ride away, leaving the other boys to wait an hour in the woods before angrily giving up.

All day, John and Jim play, losing themselves in imagination and adventure. As the day draws long, they head home toward the unfortunate turn of events, crossing paths with Tommy and Jared.

"Hey, fag boys," Jared yells out.

John can feel a lump in his throat. "Hey guys," he says, hoping not to be outed by them.

"Where you off to, Fag Land?" Tommy says, igniting the laugh of Jared, who smacks Jim in the head.

And before he can begin to peddle away, they tear him off his bike and begin kicking sand and dirt at his curled-up body. Oddly they never mess with John, for he would often hang with them.

"The police!" John calls out as the two boys turn and run into an alleyway behind some stores.

Jim gets up, disheveled and teary, wiping off dirt and dust.

"Where are the police?"

"Nowhere," John says.

"Thanks, John."

"No problem, friend," John says as he picks up Jim's bike for him.

"I hate those guys," Jim yells, sniffling his nose.

"Jerks," John says.

The two boys ride off back to Jim's basement, where they play some more and forget about the commotion.

"John, you're a good friend," Jim says as they sit on a throw rug with G.I. Joes. John smiles, and all goes black into the ethers before bright pulsating light consumes him.

"How's it feel listening to your heart?" he hears.

"It feels... well, it's not easy. Acceptance is a tricky thing. I mean surely Jim would get beat up again, I didn't prevent that."

"That is Jim's path, effects he has sown from previous actions, lessons to be learned. Every second that we are alive we are creating our lives with our actions, but that day when you led him into the woods"—suddenly Jim's wide eyes of the past are brought to light as John seems to be looking down onto that day—"you created fear and mistrust in this boy, and now you have set a new course for the boy. Never judge anyone's path. We go through what we need to in order to balance it out. We don't need to worry about affecting other's lessons. That will sort itself out. All we need do is be kind and enjoy. It's simple. And that day you did both."

Darkness again overwhelms his sight before the faint glimmer of soft snow is visible.

John seems to be floating through the soft snow, which falls like ashes from the sky toward a window where he can see himself staring out at the large, floating snow drifting in the cold air. With a flash, John opens his eyes as he folds a shirt on his bed. A quick blink brings his full attention into the room as his Blackberry vibrates on the dark oak night table.

"Hello," the middle-aged John answers.

"John, I know you're going away, and I am sorry

to be the one to rain on your parade, but the McMillian Group says they will withdraw the entire account unless you are present this week during this crisis," the voice on the phone informs.

"I understand, I'll be there," John says.

"John, this is terrible with your trip and all."

"That's the sacrifices of owning the company, Mike. We are the place of the business, and people rely on us. I'll see you tomorrow," John says hanging up the phone.

His mind quickly remembers this day. His two-week trip to Utah and California, which his family had planned all year—cancelled. Rubbing his face in the silence of his bedroom, he remembers the fallout fight he would have with Daryl. He remembers how Mallory and Sky wouldn't back him up as John tried to explain how the only reason they could ever go on a trip like this was due to his hard work and business. His rage would prompt him to leave that night to stay in his apartment in New York City to await the next day.

Sitting on the edge of the bed, he clears his mind and tries to feel his heart.

What does my heart want to do? What is the right action? he thinks. *Well of course, I'll just go away with my family. Problem solved,* he thinks. *Screw the company.*

But this still doesn't feel right in his heart.

If we lose that account I'll have to let go half of the company to make up for the account.

"This is a tough one, Old Man," he says looking at the ceiling.

Just then, Mallory walks into the room, saying, "What's that, John?"

John turns quickly with a smile. "Mal, close the door, I have to talk to you," John says softly.

"Everything, okay, John?" she asks, sitting on the beige comforter that drapes off the large bed. "Baby?" she probes as John stares blankly.

"Mallory, there's an issue at work. The McMillian Group is in litigation as you know, and their accounts are, well, don't let me bore you with semantics. Long story short, if we want to keep them as a client, I need to be there this week or they'll pull the account."

"John," Mallory says with a look of disappointment.

"I know, I mean, if I don't go, we lose half the company."

"And if you do, you still have your family, but you will lose part of them for sure, at least mentally. John, we don't spend time with the kids as it is."

"I know," a tear drops down his face.

"Tell Sky and Daryl to meet us in the family room in fifteen minutes. I promise I will make this right.

Mallory nods. "What are you gonna tell them? I mean, I'm used to this, but the kids?"

John grasps Mallory's upper arms and stares completely into her eyes, "Baby, I'm sorry. I never meant to," he whispers past a knot in his throat.

"I know, John, but you did."

Mallory turns and leaves the room, leaving John, who stands in the seeming emptiness of his mind. John turns to look out the window. He attempts to still his spinning mind and listen to his heart, and after ten minutes he leaves the room, descending the stairs to the family room. Sky stands with folded arms, her red- streaked brown hair falls from her shoulders. Daryl sits with head in hand scratching his short, curly, dark-blonde hair as he looks up to greet his father.

"So, I've called this meeting because I have something to share with you all. It seems something has come up, on matters of extreme importance for the company, and it seems I won't be able to make it away with you guys this week."

"What?" Daryl yells out.

"Somehow we are never of extreme importance or any importance for that matter," Sky mumbles.

"No baby, you are, and I realize I've been an ass

and haven't done my family the justice they deserve."

Daryl stands up. "You're such a jerk. Always Dad's way! What the fuck!"

"Hey, watch your mouth," Mallory scolds.

"Dad, your family is in New York City. Go be with them."

It's at this point John remembers feeling this anger, but he breathes it away and proceeds with his heart, knowing Daryl says this only out of pain.

"Daryl, please hear me out." Daryl sits again, face red with anger. "I have decided I haven't been the father I should be. So go to Utah tomorrow, have fun, and I will fly out for the weekend, and going forward I want each of you to pick a place to go and we will go four times a year, as a family, and nothing will come between us. If I am not there this week many people will lose their jobs. It's not that you're not important. You are the most important to me, but I have a responsibility to the workers and their families. I ask you to please forgive me and to trust that I promise to spend more time, true quality time, from this moment on."

He walks over to Mallory, who smiles, surprised with how he has handled this.

"Sky, hon, listen, I'll let you all decide, like a jury. And if you decide I stay and go with you tomorrow, I will. Take a few minutes to decide."

John walks out through the French doors in the back of the room, waiting in the kitchen as he brews a pot of coffee.

Sky walks in, "Okay, Daddy, we've made a decision. We feel, because of the people who work for you, it's important you be there, and we'll see you this weekend."

John smiles.

"But I already know where my place will be," she says still stone-faced.

"Where's that baby?" John asks as the rest of the family walks into the room.

"Greece!" She yells out, as they enter behind her, laughing.

John ascends his body, and all falls completely black.

"You give your family a lot, John," he hears in the darkness.

"All but myself," he answers with ill content.

"My wealth can give them trips and things, but I remember simpler times."

Often money costs too much, John thinks as he reflects on those with simpler lives and modest incomes who are able to spend time with their families.

"John, even those with modest incomes struggle to make time for loved ones, even more so often. It's a choice you must make." he hears from the old man.

"I agree," John concurs.

"Time, John. What price can you affix to time?"

"None," he says as a wind howls in the darkness and small white dots pass his gaze.

The dots are blurry at first, but as he blinks, they come into view, and as his gaze zooms out, he sits as a young boy in his childhood living room staring at the heavy snow that falls in the dark night.

"Father," he whispers as he watches his father decorate a tree he so fondly remembers to be the last his father ever would.

A record player softly etches the sounds of Frank Sinatra Christmas music. John inhales the smell of homemade cookies as his sister joyfully enters.

"And cookies," his mother sings placing down a plate of freshly baked sugar and chocolate chip cookies. Marissa sings, following her mother with two tall glasses of milk.

John is in awe as his heart wells up. *We didn't have much,* he thinks, but we had each other, and the time we spent together was priceless.

"Well if it isn't the two most beautiful women in the known existence," John's father says, donning a Santa hat as he sits on the couch next to John.

John remembers how his father would always say this, and it brought a smile to his face as he picked up a cookie.

"So, what did you ask Santa for Christmas?" John's father asks.

"I want a record player and a new piano," Marissa blurts out.

"But you have a record player and a piano."

"But I want my own, so I can listen in my room."

Her mother smiles at their father, knowing they already got her one stowed away in the closet.

"Well a piano may be too big to fit on that sleigh of his," her father answers.

John's bite cuts the cookie as a rush of nostalgia floods his mind.

"No one makes 'em like you, Mom," he says as she smiles back with a quick caress of his heart.

"Santa brought Mrs. Dunkin a car last year. It's a magic sled, you know?" Marissa says as they all laugh.

"And you, John," his father says, placing his hand

on John's thigh.

John holds back tears of love and admiration; he had forgotten how much he loved his father, a love suppressed in decades of rage.

"I already have everything I would ever ask for right here in this room," he says.

Taken aback, his father smiles at their mother.

"Kiss up," Marissa whispers, thinking he is buttering them up for more presents.

"Well this isn't going to decorate itself," John's father says standing as John watches them all grab ornaments.

With a glass of milk in one hand and a cookie in another, he feels overjoyed as a pause in the record brings on "Have Yourself a Merry Little Christmas." The warmth of joy overcomes him as a tear slides down his cheek.

"What am I to do here?" he asks the old man in his mind.

"Simply enjoy and be present. It's all we can ever do," he hears in his mind.

"Through the years we all will be together," Sinatra sings as he watches, completely present, enveloped in joy.

He begins to lift from his boyhood body and passes

through Marissa toward the snowy night. As he drifts like a piece of snow far from the house, he remembers how although his memories of his father were often daunting, sad ones, the beautiful memories such as that night could easily trump any sadness.

"Your father is what you created him to be. You choose what to focus on, you choose the memories that create him."

"But the hard times, the times he was horrible?"

"We're human, John, and although we can't control how others perceive us, we can do our best to be good examples. Which memories do you wish your children to remember as you?"

And with that, all falls dark and silent.

the
eleventh
chapter

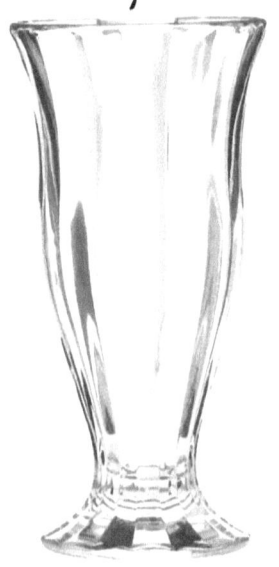

Rain falls heavily on a metal cover, where a young John stores away, squatting in his suit and black tie, holding his knees, pressed up against his damp dog, Rusty, who consoles this lonely and confused boy.

"John? John!" he hears from the back door the voice of his aunt, his mother's sister, calling him in from the yard.

John is secure in his metal-covered cubical far from the sadness of the post funeral gathering in his house.

"John boy, come on, love," she now says, standing in the rain as drops smash heavy on the ground, soaking past her patent-leather black shoes to her stockings.

Slowly he comes out and holds close to his aunt as the umbrella tries valiantly to shelter them. They scurry toward the house, followed by Rusty, and enter the back room, devoid of family. His aunt kneels down, her ruddy face and curly reddish- brown hair frizzed from the rain. John remembers her smell, that perfume she would wear, almost nauseating, yet comforting.

"John, I know this is tough for you, but you must understand it is tough on your mother as well," his aunt says with soft compassion.

John now remembers how he had stormed out of the house in anger at his mom. From this day on he would blame her for his father's death. He would blame his father for his mother's sadness, and even as he got older, and this seemed silly, the unconscious child would hold this view into adulthood.

Tears fill John's eyes as his aunt wipes them with a handkerchief.

"Your mother needs your love more than ever, John," she says.

John remembers hearing those words, but until now they never made complete sense. Somehow those words penetrate the very depths of his heart as he begins to cry even harder, his aunt still kneeling holds him close.

"We all love you dearly, John, but one here loves you most, and she is right in there."

John gathers himself and slowly walks into the living room. He remembers the somber tone of the room. He remembers how on the outside everyone pretended to have it all together, but how he could feel their screaming pain on the inside. *Liars! All liars!* He remembers thinking. Slowly, he makes his way over to his mother and realizes how deeply he wants to forgive her. He can feel her immense suffering under the veil of a false smile and vows that instead of being rebellious he will comfort her, the healing power of regret versus guilt. He slowly draws near her, and as she realizes his presence, she gives a half smile, covering her pain as he quickly latches to her tightly.

"I'm sorry, Mom, I'm sorry," he mutters through the tears.

"John, it's not your fault, baby. You have nothing to be sorry for."

These words she says illuminate a deep sense of blaming: he blamed himself as well as his mother. He peeks out from the damp dress he pulls his teary face from and smiles at his aunt, who looks like a glorified angel standing in the kitchen.

Slowly he pulls out of his body, and as he ascends the dark party, he notices Marissa on the couch.

She looks like the saddest girl in the world, he thinks. My selfishness and blame never let me be there for them.

You were but a child, a confused child, he hears.

"Yes, now I am able to realize this, but as I leave that child, will he regress back?" John wonders.

"You have set an intention; one action sets in place all that proceeds from it. John, you change your fate with every thought, every action, every word. Most important, every intention."

"I felt the guilt lift from my being as I held my mother close. Years of buried guilt I didn't even know was there," John says.

"Why is that, do you think? Why did the guilt dissipate?"

"I guess I felt guilty not being able to comfort her, not being there for her when she needed me. Even though I was a boy and had my own confusion, I realized that we can all time travel, Old Man."

"How so?"

"Once we release the guilt of what we have done in the past, we can use regret to resolve never to do it again. I felt as if guilt only weakened me and created pain in my life even if only on an unconscious level, but the regret, the resolve, made me strong, and in any moment anyone can do this. I just wish I had realized this sooner. So much guilt, Old Man, so much useless guilt."

"You realize it now, John, don't fret. Your realization that you can change your past by changing your thoughts is immense, and one I assure you that is not for naught. Some people go their entire lives with guilt about something and often do the same things that created the guilt, just in different forms. You now have learned that your resolve, your regret, can be a powerful transformational tool and one that can awaken your responsibility to the kindness and joy in the world."

And with that John's heart flutters as a white light permeates his view.

*the
twelfth
chapter*

John's eyes adjust as the smell of the hot dirt under his feet draws his awareness to this very unfamiliar world. Palm trees line a quiet dirt road where he stands before a seaside home with streaks of washed-out white paint across the wood-paneled front, holding up a steep-sloped roof.

Where am I? he wonders.

The air is silent, with only a whisper of evening bugs in the distance. Palm fronds wave in the light breeze as John stands unassuming.

"Hello? Old Man, I think there's been a mistake," he yells out to the sky.

"No mistake," he hears echoing back. "Go inside, John."

"Whose house is this?"

"No one you know. Just open the door and don't worry, they can't see you."

John places his hand on the door handle. As his heart flutters he slowly turns the warm metal knob, creaking it open, and steps inside the dimly lit house with dark, wood-planked floors. A slim and dark Asian woman hurries past him with a washbowl and towels, confirming that she can't see him, as she doesn't even look at him in her scurry.

"What am I doing here?" he whispers.

"Go to the room," he hears.

"What room?"

"Follow her."

He can hear a commotion, as if a woman is being harmed. He hesitates before walking down the hall. The door of the room is ajar. A dust-specked stream of light directs him into the room.

A woman lies in sweat-soaked sheets as a hunching man seems to be directing her to push. The woman, who scurried past him earlier, wipes the lying woman's brow with a damp cloth and gives her instructions in a foreign language. She seems to be trying to calm her. As the sweating woman's face turns red, beads of sweat pop from her brow, and she breathlessly pushes, emitting a baby into the man's awaiting hands. He slowly pulls before reaching for a tool laid out on a white cloth on the floor.

The man wipes sweat from his brow with a swipe of his forearm before cutting the umbilical cord. Using another instrument, he clears the mucus from the newborn as if he has done this a thousand times before. Just then, the baby cries out in sweet disarray, a harmonious scream that on any other occasion would be troublesome. John stands in awe of new life.

"Amazing!" he whispers, having only seen this twice before, once in his eighth-grade biology class, on an old film leaving all the students disgusted and uncomfortable, and again when his daughter, Sky, was born—a moment he wept with joy in an unexplainable feeling of bliss and terror.

"Go down the hall to the room at the other end of the house," he hears the old man say.

John is confused why he is here, but goes along with his instructions because he feels a trust for the old man now. The woman now holds her baby with an exhausted smile as the other woman cleans up the floor. The doctor offers words bedside, with a seeming look of concern on his face.

"Where am I?" John asks, as he stands watching the scene play out in front of him.

"Malaysia, John. It will all make sense in a moment. Proceed to the room at the other end of the house."

John walks out from the room, well lit from the evening sun, and adjusts his eyes in the dim hallway, proceeding to the end of the creaky wood floor. Stopping at the front door he can see another room just a few feet ahead.

"Go on," he hears.

As he enters the room, the cheer of new birth energy is diluted by the somber heaviness of tears. A young boy sits against the wall, holding his darkly tanned knees to his chest, watching a frail man lying on a slim mattress on the floor.

"What's the matter here?" he asks.

"That's the newborn's brother, and the man on the bed is their father."

"Why is he crying?"'

"His father is dying—leukemia."

"That's horrible," John says as a lump swells in his throat.

A thick silence seems to permeate his entire existence.

"I'm sorry. I don't know why I am here. I mean, it's amazing how this is possible, but I am excited and sad and just a mix of confusion here. If there is something to be learned, I am not exactly sure what," John says, staring at the frail man lying still in beads of sweat that seem to grow from his pale face.

"Would you like to know how he got leukemia,

John?"

"I guess so."

"There is a factory not far from here. In fact, you could walk there in about ten minutes. They deal in the refinement of rare earths, in particular neodymium. Ever heard of it?" the old man asks as he materializes into the room and stares at the man on the bed.

"Whoa, there you are," John says, taken aback. "Yeah, I have actually heard of it."

"Yes, you have, haven't you? Well in order to extract this rare earth, which will be shipped to China to create parts for smart phones, a great deal of radioactive and toxic waste is produced. Do you know how they dispose of that waste, John?"

"No, no I don't," John says as he looks up, face now ridden with guilt.

"Well, the companies that invest in this process know that proper waste disposal is very costly, and since bottom line is of the utmost with them, then neither do they. They turn a blind eye as waste is given to the local farmers and told it is fertilizer or to others who are told it is quicklime, and the rest is dumped into the South China Sea."

"That's horrible!" John exclaims, looking over at the old man.

"Some would say that's horrible, others would say it's smart business."

"Is that how this man got leukemia?" John asks in concern.

"This man was given free quicklime. In fact, he painted his house with it as it kept away the mosquitoes and rats. The food this family has been eating for years now is induced with toxic and radioactive waste without them even knowing this. So I can only assume that this is one case of many here in the village that is due to this blatant irresponsibility of a company that failed to look at the details."

"That's horrible," John whispers.

"He will be dead in about three days. His new-born son will never know his father. And what's more, his newborn son is practically blind and mentally retard-ed as a result of this waste, one of many children here in this village being born with severe disabilities. John, what monsters would do such a thing?"

"I don't know," John says as he looks up at a mirror and sees his face.

"John, do you know who is responsible for this?"

"Old Man, I know where this is going. Not too long ago we invested in that tech company that worked in rare earths in Malaysia to create smart phones in China, but I assure you I had no idea of the magnitude of this."

"Of course not, John. At an almost thousand-percent return on investment, the details need not be disclosed."

John looks at the old man with a mix of anger and disgust veiled in guilt, saying, "Old Man, please! I am not to blame for this. I couldn't have known."

"You are partially right, John. Today corporations sort of take on a life of their own where even the CEO is a slave to the bottom line, to the stockholders, and returns and growth of a company. Greed has become a normal way of conducting business, and we don't even see it as wrong, in the corporate world. It's an accepted way of doing business now. The CEO is responsible for growth at whatever cost, regardless of the moral responsibility, right, John?"

"Well, Old Man, I never intended to hurt or kill anyone, I swear it."

"I know, John. I am not here to punish you or condemn you."

"So then why do you show me this?"

"Maybe to open your eyes a bit. There is a deep

denial of responsibility here in the world, John, and it is growing exponentially. We pretend to be advanced and intelligent, yet our actions are no more than animalistic, based on survival. The biggest and the best corporations survive no matter what the cost, the environmental devastation, the harm to humanity and other animals."

John hangs his head in disgust knowing he has made many deals in this fashion.

"The thing is, John, the corporation will never make enough money, and so the health of a human being or the environment is easily passed by in this insatiable desire to keep growing and making more money. It's a collective effort here that starts with each consumer up to the CEO and even those who run the factories here in Malaysia."

The young boy rises up and walks off out of the room. As John watches him pass, he can feel the sullen despair of the boy.

"It seems like a runaway train, like it's too far gone and too much of the normal way of conducting business. How could it ever be turned around now? It is so hard even to point a finger when we all have a hand in this," John frets.

"And within this system if a CEO chooses to help protect environmental or human interests at the cost of profits, he will surely be fired for one who will not, right?" the old man asks.

"Absolutely. It's a dog-eat-dog world out there, Old Man, we are doomed!"

"Don't be so grim, John. You are the owner of your company. No one can fire you but you. It's your own drive for more that dictates your actions here."

"I have stockholders and board members to worry about too. I am far from the boss in the grand scheme of things."

"We all want this fictitious character to blame, don't we, John? Perhaps some fat suit sitting in a high tower in Manhattan, on a golden recliner, barking orders at his minions. But the truth is that this does not exist. The fat man is the collective, our collective choices from each employee to every consumer, all the way up to you and your partners, after all, you are just working from the demand of the consumer, aren't you?"

"Yes, of course. Yet, I feel the demands are often dictated by commercialism telling us what to think, do, have, and be."

"True, but everyone has the ability to think for themselves. You taught this to your children, didn't you? How not to believe all the hype and to see through the commercialism of things and think for themselves didn't you?"

"I did," John says as he kneels by the man lying still.

"Come, John. It's time to leave this place."

"But—"

All falls dark and fades away as they ascend above the house slowly pulling away from this sleepy seaside town in Malaysia.

"We must all take responsibility individually, and only then can we begin to change the collective. It must start with ourselves. What could you have done differently, John?"

"A lot," he whispers in the dark silence.

the
thirteenth
chapter

"John. John?"

His vision adjusts to a boardroom where he sits in a suit with five others.

"John?" a woman asks.

"Yeah, hey, sorry, I zoned out there. Been a little under the weather," he lies.

"Well, here is the proposal, and we would be fools not to jump on this: the risks are low, and the potential income is immense. One thousand percent in the first quarter alone," a man at the head of the table speaks.

John looks down at the thick packet that lies next to his legal pad with notes jotted on it.

The Malaysia deal, he inwardly notes.

"And for the people?" John interrupts.

"What people?" a woman with pin-straight brown hair and neatly pressed suit asks.

"The people who live in the village adjacent to the factories," he goes on.

"They will be the first ones to be able to take advantage of the job opportunities we will be creating for them," the man at the head goes on. "It's a win-win."

"Article 16B," John says flipping in the packet, "waste removal. We have no idea what these chemicals will do, and we'll just take our chances putting it in the soil of these unsuspecting people?"

They look at John curiously.

"John, it's safe. We'll deal with that when it presents itself," the man says.

"No, John has a valid point. We don't need the lawsuits and the bad press. All we need is some quixotic Peace Corps student to take up the issue and lead a revolt, painting a bad image," another young, suited man points out.

"And then our bad image, our lawsuits? What about poisoning men, woman, and children?" John asks.

"At a thousand percent returns on investment, we can afford a lawsuit," an older gentleman with thick glasses interjects.

"Say, Marshal," John begins, directed at the older gentleman with thick glasses, "perhaps we can test it here first, maybe that woods behind your house on Long Island. Your wife wouldn't mind if potentially dangerous and life-threatening chemicals joined her water supply, would she? I mean your kids are all grown up, so its only grandkids you'd worry for."

Marshal's face grows red as he looks at John.

"When did you become Saint John?" Marshal asks.

"I'm not a saint. Far from it, but my company will not invest in the suffering of others due to an ignorant one-thousand percent return," John says.

"When you play at our level, you create a massive amount of good with some bad. It's how it goes John," Marshal explains. "We'll invest in more charity, cleaning systems for the village water, things of this sort."

"Bullshit! Because if we did, then our thousand-percent turns to a hundred percent, and then why not just do it in the States? It's the easy removal of chemicals that makes this deal sweet, but today my new nose smells that old scent of drama, and it stinks! They'll be other investments, this one I will say pass. Thank you all for the opportunity," John says rising up and leaving the boardroom, proceeding to his office.

As he sits at his desk, he notices he hasn't moved on to the next scene, *still must be more to do,* he thinks.

A woman enters his office, "Valiant, John, I respect that."

John seems still troubled. "This investment will go on to the Rocksford Corporation, and of course they will fund it," John says, feeling defeated.

"But at least we didn't," she says. "And we can pass this info along to the press and my friend at the U.N., to almost ensure it doesn't happen without safe waste management."

"I would have taken the deal and cut out profits to ensure safe waste management, but I don't want to engage in a company that deals in the devastation of others," John says.

"John, you hit your head on the way in?" the woman laughs.

"We do what we can, Jan," John says with a smile, as he pulls out of his body.

We do what we can with what we have, he hears.

"How do I know that the other John won't instantly jolt up and rehash that deal, thinking a moment of insanity overcame him?" he asks the old man as he pulls away.

"Interesting thing when you show someone what their heart really wants to do: you change the world, you changed your brain chemistry, the thinking process. Old John does not even exist. In fact you have dramatically changed Jan's life for the better as well. That impression alone has sparked inspiration in a way you could not fathom."

"Will I ever see you again, Old Man, or are you acting as my conscious from now on?"

"Patience, John, patience," he hears, as all sounds fade into birds chirping in the distance.

John sits at the pond fishing with Bill on that day he had last seen him. The peace of Baldwin Pond overcomes him as Bill casts out.

"...Liz McCullen," Bill says with a silent laugh rolling out from an obvious conversation before John's awareness was fully present.

"Liz," he replies back, to suggest he's still in the conversation.

"Anyway, John, there's something I need to tell you."

John already knows what's coming next, and his wisdom of regret mixes with the young John's anger, anticipating a fight and disappointment.

"What's that, Bill?"

"I'm leaving school, John," Bill says seriously.

Anger wells up in John, mixed with disappointment. He can feel sarcasm rising. Cynicism fills his mind. His heart struggles to be heard in the chaos and noise of a deluded mind.

"Hmmmmm," John simply casts out. *What do I do?* he thinks.

Allow yourself to feel the pain of anger, the disappointment, don't run from it, he hears in his mind.

You can always stop, it's hard not to react, but the more you just stop and don't let the anger control you, then the situation does not have to be created out of your insecure anger. It's obvious you didn't like the result. So stop and think, "How would I like to handle this? What result do I wish to produce?" And proceed accordingly, no matter how strong the pull of anger is.

"John?" Bill says as John stares almost blankly.

"And what would you do a thing like that for, Bill?"

Bill goes on to explain his hopes and dreams and plans to travel to India to a silent John who reels with no intention of catching a fish but to hear the gentle spool of fishing line, as his anger lifts.

"Bill, I'd be lying if I said I wasn't upset and disappointed."

"I know John, I know. I want you to be happy, to follow your bliss but I need you to understand this is not mine," Bill says.

John's heart now leads a conversation.

"Bill, I do understand. My anger and disappointment comes from a deep sense of need and want. I hope you understand," John says.

"John, of course I do, and I will still put you in contact with my father and his associates when the time arises."

"I know you will, Bill. I'll miss you, buddy," John says, knowing there is really not much for him to do but accept his friend and his dreams.

"John, I promise you this, not only will we see each other, but perhaps I'll make some international contacts for you."

John smiles and realizes that oddly this path of least effort and acceptance may actually benefit him more than he thought, but the primary thing is that he is respecting and maintaining a friendship he always regretted losing.

"The world is our oyster, John," Bill smiles as a snag pulls his line. "Whoa! Got one," he yells as John looks on in wonder slowly pulling out above them as he watches two friends revel in a moment of great happiness.

Further he pulls until he sees only shapes and colors, a feeling of perfection and order fills him as he hears a whisper, "All is in perfect order and harmony, yet we choose how to experience it."

A deep blue floods his vision with sparkling green flakes that shudder with speed and zap his mind, shutting his eyes with a quiet solitude of peace.

the
fourteenth
chapter

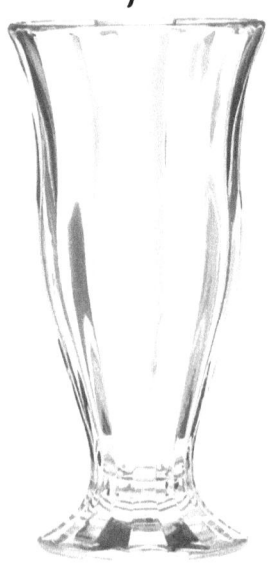

A ten-year-old John stands in the dirt street in front of his house in dark blue jeans, kicking dust in frustrated boredom. The hot summer sun begins to dissipate in the distant, puffy-white clouds. Sweat from a day's play has dried dirt to his tanned face, which stands out atop his dirty white t-shirt. His eyes perk up as a 1963 Oxford Blue Ford Galaxie 500 comes slowly down the road. It's his father. He remembers when he bought that car new three years before, against his mother's wishes, using the only savings they had. As he pulls up, arm hanging on the open window, he exudes a coolness that John remembers well.

"Where's your Mom?" his father asks with a smile.

"Inside, she's really sore you know."

"I know," he says staring at the house.

"Why'd you do it, Pop?" John asks, alluding to the drunken fight, ending with him smacking his mother and her kicking him out.

"Get in, John, I want to show you something."

John gets in the car, feeling an anger that if he were a bit bigger he would punch his father right in the nose for hurting his mother. The ride is silent, with the occasional smile from his father. He can smell the stale booze from the night before among the cigarette stink that permanently lives in the car and will remain there even after he has passed away. He remembers how much *brian e. miller*

his father loved that car, often accused by his wife that he loved it more than her, an accusation John never believed, for he knows, that among the fights and delusions, his father always loved her. They slowly pull up to a cliff overlooking the Sound.

The sun has begun its perfect decent, beginning a show of tangerine streaks that give way to streams of pink clouds that turn deep purple before their eyes. John realizes that within this moment of silence his father is communicating with him. Although he never told him that he loved him, he knows at this moment it is exactly what he is doing.

"You know I love your Mother," he says breaking the silence.

"I know," John says, suddenly feeling a deep sense of understanding for the pain and suffering his father has constantly battled.

From this day on he would drink more and more, driving himself further away from his family, and within a year he would die in a drunken accident, after yet another epic fight over absolutely nothing at all.

Why? John asks inside.

We cannot question the order: the Universe has a perfect accounting system. No debt goes unpaid, and all is in perfect order, he hears.

After the sun danced it's final rays of beauty from under the horizon of the Long Island Sound from where it now sleeps, they drive off in silence. Arriving back at the house, John's father gets out as his mother stands in the doorway looking out through the screened door.

"I'll be back soon, John. Gonna spend the night at Michael's."

John grabs his father and holds him tighter than he has ever remembered. As he gets into his car, John calls out, "I love you, Dad" as a tear falls down his face.

John's father smiles, "I know you do, son," and drives away.

John stands in the dusky road as dust clouds the dimly lit path where his father has driven off. A knot in his throat holds back the tears. He forgives his father, not for the pain he caused them all, not for hitting his mother, but for the delusions that caused him to do this. And at that moment he realizes that it is himself that he had forgiven. He wasn't letting his father off the hook, he was letting himself off, realizing the power his past had over him that caused him to destroy friendships and, perhaps most important, his relationship with his mother.

Turning to the house, he sees his mother still standing in the silence of the now pale moonrise and as he nears, the door's metal coils slowly invite him to his still silent mother. He quickly grabs his mother around her waist, remembering the sweet smell of honeysuckles and baking she exudes. His mother never made John play sides, she always accepted him as he was. Weeping he realizes that he always judged and threw himself on sides, all the while his mother's love stayed constant and undying. John's tears fall uncontrollably as his mother simply holds his head, pressing his cheek against her apron. John vows to learn from his mother's equanimity and constant love, unscorned by judgment.

"I love you, Mom," he says in the gargle of tears in his throat.

"I know, John Boy. I love you more than all the stars in the sky, baby," John weeps again, knowing that is a vast understatement.

"Come on, John, your dinner's getting cold. Go wash up."

John does as he was told, surprised he hasn't left this scene yet. Coming to the table, Marissa sits as John remembers the peace and love that their mother emitted even in the seeming worst of times. Slowly he pulls out of his body, ascending the small dinner party, through the roof, way up into the stars, as he becomes the light of the brightest star, the vast brightness flashing him into an emptiness of unexplainable bliss.

I'm dead, he thinks, as in that moment thoughts don't even seem to make sense as all that exists is the warmth of love and unbounded bliss.

the

final

chapter

Soft embers burn away the afternoon chill within the fireplace upstairs. John opens his eyes blinking away the flashes of sweet light he vaguely remembers. He sits up on the large bed still in a bathrobe but the clock reads 1:42.

Where am I? he wonders.

The mirror reflects a John, the eldest he could remember, the age he had a heart attack, but rubbing his face he looks less stressed and even a bit tan, an oddity as it's clearly winter out. A picture of he and Mallory set on the nightstand, he remembers not the beachy scene it reflects, although they look elated.

"Where am I?" he asks with no answer.

"John, come on. They're here," he hears Mallory call up.

He slowly makes his way toward the door, adjusting the white, long robe that covers his flannel pajamas. Making his way downstairs, he notices his mother as she comes in the door.

She looks great. Still alive, he thinks in wonder.

"Oh, John, get dressed," Mallory giggles.

"Merry Christmas, John," his mother says, followed by a man with gray hair carrying bags of presents.

"I'm staying in pajamas too, Dad," Darryl says from atop the stairs.

John looks up and laughs. "Wonderful," he yells out as he clears the last step with a hop of delight.

"Mom," he says, holding back tears that begin to well up as he gives a lasting, strong hug.

"Hey, I'm John," he says extending a hand to the curious man beside his mother who hands John a bag of presents.

"Yeah, and I'm Santa Claus, happy Christmas, John, hey Mal," he says giving her a kiss on her cheek.

"Hey, Maurice. Merry merry," she returns.

"Burrr, close the door," Mallory says as they all file into the large house John doesn't recognize but oddly feels comfortable in.

"Come on, John. Really, your sister will be here soon," Mallory says before kissing his cheek.

As he watches her walk away, he wonders at how much he truly loves her and reflects on the day they met and he told her that she was the piece of the puzzle that perfectly fit his.

What's this all about? he wonders, standing in the lower family room.

The fire crackles as he looks out the window and squints.

"Old Man," he says out loud, noticing the old

man is standing in the yard in front of the evergreen trees that fall into the forest behind the estate.

Sliding the glass door open, he makes his way out in his slippers as the joyful chatter in the kitchen fades. The sky is clouded grey, the air a damp cold, as small snow flurries begin to fall from the sky. The smiling old man beckons him near with his blue eyes.

"What's this about, Old Man?"

"Life, John."

"What's that?"

"This is your life, the result of choices made."

"But it's not. It's different."

"Who is Maurice?" he asks.

The old man laughs.

"He is your stepfather, John. Your acceptance allowed your mother to heal and love again. Your more successful financially as well, but your investment firm, it never happened or rather it did but not in this possibility of infinites."

"What do I do?"

"You and Bill opened a sustainable energy company, really cutting edge. J & B Energy is a household name."

"And my father?" John asks with concern.

"Some things happen, and we think it's for the worst, but it's simply part of the perfection. He passed as you remember. He was a great teacher to you in many ways." The old man pauses, then goes on. "Yet a child was born to your family not long after his passing."

"What's that got to do with anything?" John asks.

"Oh no bother. John, this is a life of great wonder, joy, and love: the two lives streaming juxtaposed one atop the other in the realm of infinite possibilities of experience that sets upon the perfection of life, and here you are, always."

"But I'll have to adapt, that's for sure, so much to learn", John says as the snow begins to fall about heavier, floating in various directions.

"John," the old man begins, holding up his hand. "When I snap my fingers you won't remember anything that has happened in the past few days. You will simply accept this life as it always has been, naturally and wholly.

John smiles and just as he begins to snap, he yells, "Wait! Who are you, Old Man?"

Smiling as snow thickens in its descent the old man says, "I'm you, John. I am the greatest potential of your highest self. And like all things, I will pass, but each second is a chance to create peace and joy and positive change in the world."

And then, "Snap!"

The snow falls hard, and as John stands alone in the yard he can hear "Have Yourself a Merry Little Christmas" playing from the house as all falls pure white.

the end...

www.ingramcontent.com/pod-product-compliance
Lightning Source LLC
Chambersburg PA
CBHW020150180626
46810CB00004B/1827